PUFFIN BOOKS

Fat Puss and Slimpup

Harriet Castor grew up in Warwickshire, where she went to a full-time dancing school. She has been writing stories for as long as she can remember, and wrote her first Puffin book, *Fat Puss and Friends*, at the age of twelve. After graduating from Cambridge University with a degree in History, she lived in Prague for a while, teaching English and getting lost on trams. Now back in Britain, she works as an editor in children's publishing and writes books in her spare time. She lives in London with a nice person called John but – much to her disappointment – no cat.

KV-192-801

Also by Harriet Castor

FAT PUSS AND FRIENDS
FAT PUSS ON WHEELS

Fat Puss
and Slimpup

Harriet Castor

Illustrated by
Colin West

PUFFIN BOOKS

To Will and Johnny B.

PUFFIN BOOKS

Published by the Penguin Group
Penguin Books Ltd, 27 Wrights Lane, London W8 5TZ, England
Penguin Books USA Inc., 375 Hudson Street, New York, New York 10014, USA
Penguin Books Australia Ltd, Ringwood, Victoria, Australia
Penguin Books Canada Ltd, 10 Alcorn Avenue, Toronto, Ontario, Canada M4V 3B2
Penguin Books (NZ) Ltd, 182–190 Wairau Road, Auckland 10, New Zealand

Penguin Books Ltd, Registered Offices: Harmondsworth, Middlesex, England

First published by Viking 1994
Published in Puffin Books 1995
3 5 7 9 10 8 6 4 2

Text copyright © Harriet Castor, 1994
Illustrations copyright © Colin West, 1994
All rights reserved

The moral right of the author and illustrator has been asserted

Printed in England by Clays Ltd, St Ives plc

Except in the United States of America, this book is sold subject
to the condition that it shall not, by way of trade or otherwise, be lent,
re-sold, hired out, or otherwise circulated without the publisher's
prior consent in any form of binding or cover other than that in
which it is published and without a similar condition including this
condition being imposed on the subsequent purchaser

Contents

Fat Puss and Slimpup

It was a clear blue day in autumn. Fat Puss had just wandered out into the morning sun when he saw the Mouse family heading his way.

"Hello there!" called
Terence Mouse. "We were just
coming to see you."

"Oh good!" said Fat Puss.
"Are you off on a trip?"

"Well, sort of," said Jessica.

"We're going cherry
picking!" said Charlotte
excitedly.

"Yes," said Terence. "We're
going to help Humphrey
Beaver pick the cherries on his

cherry tree, and we thought
you might like to come and
help us."

"Picking cherries?" said Fat
Puss, who hadn't realized that
cherries grew on trees. "That
sounds fun. But would
Humphrey mind?"

"Not at all," replied Jessica. "We must pick the cherries now because they're just ready to eat, and if we leave them they'll fall off the branches and get spoilt. The more help we have, the quicker the job will get done."

"Yes, and the quicker we can eat the cherries!" said Charlotte Mouse.

"And make them into cherry tarts and cherry jam," added Robert.

"Oh, that sounds lovely," said Fat Puss, who liked cherry tarts and cherry jam very much.

So they set off to find Humphrey's cherry tree. When they got there, they saw that the tree was heavy with lots and lots of dark red, shiny fruit.

"Ooh, don't they look lovely?" chirped the baby crows, who had come along to help too.

"Now, no eating yet," laughed Grandma Crow, "or there'll be none left for tea."

Humphrey fetched his ladder
and propped it against the tree.

"Who's going up to get the
ones at the top?" he asked.

"I will!" said Fat Puss,
feeling rather brave all of a
sudden.

He started to climb the
ladder. But as he got higher,
he began to feel a bit less brave
and a lot more wobbly.

"Hang on a minute, Fat Puss!" called Humphrey suddenly. "The ladder's getting rather bendy. Perhaps you'd better come down."

"Oh, all right," said Fat Puss, trying not to sound relieved.

"Never mind," said Jessica, who thought he might be disappointed. "You can help even more down here. If I climb on your shoulders, I'll be able to reach the lower branches.

"That's a good idea," said Fat Puss.

So they all set to work.

The Crow family flew back and forth, picking bunches of fruit and delivering them to the baskets.

Humphrey held the ladder steady while Terence and Charlotte took it in turns to go up to the top branches.

Jessica and Robert clambered up on to Fat Puss to reach the branches further down.

It was tiring work, and soon
they were all looking forward
to their tea.

At last they had finished.
Humphrey took down the
ladder and they all went off to
sit by the river and dangle their
tired feet in the water.

"I wonder how many baskets we've filled?" said Humphrey after a while.

"I'll go and count them," offered Fat Puss.

So he went back to have a look in the baskets. But, to his surprise, he found that instead of being full to the top with the lovely red cherries, most of them were half empty. Some

baskets didn't have any
cherries in at all.

"That's strange," said Fat
Puss to himself. "I'm sure we
picked lots and lots. Where can
they have got to?"

Just then he heard a strange, snuffly, snory noise coming from behind the baskets. Then he spotted a trail of cherry-red paw prints on the ground.

He followed them round,
and there, nestled up against
the baskets, his paws clutching
his tummy, was a small dog
with short legs and very large
ears.

As Fat Puss stared at him,
the dog opened his eyes.
"Hello – who are you?" he
asked.

"I'm Fat Puss," said Fat
Puss.

"I'm Slimpup," said the dog.
"And I'm VERY full. Would
you like some of my cherries?"

"*Your* cherries?" asked Fat
Puss, suddenly wondering

whether he'd found the right tree and the right baskets after all.

"Yes," said Slimpup. "I found them. Someone had left them out here. They didn't want them. So I couldn't let them go to waste."

"Oh, but somebody *did* want them," said Fat Puss sadly, realizing what had happened.

"Somebody did?" said Slimpup, startled. "Who?"

"Me," said Fat Puss. "I mean us. We've all just picked them."

"So you hadn't forgotten them?" asked Slimpup. Fat Puss shook his head.

"Oh dear," said Slimpup, frowning. "I've been a very bad dog. Are you awfully cross?" He looked up at Fat Puss worriedly.

"Cross?" said Fat Puss,
surprised. "No – it wasn't your
fault. It's just that we were all
rather looking forward to
having cherry tarts and cherry
jam for tea." Slimpup hung his
head. "But don't worry," said
Fat Puss, smiling. "You must
come and meet the others."

"Are you sure that's a good idea?" asked Slimpup anxiously.

"Of course it is," said Fat Puss.

So Fat Puss took Slimpup to meet Humphrey, the mice and the crows. They were all so excited to meet a new friend that they didn't mind about the cherries at all.

"Never mind," said
Humphrey. "We must have tea
anyway – to welcome
Slimpup."

When the time came for tea,
they even found that there
were enough cherries left in the
bottom of the baskets to make
one pot of cherry jam and one
cherry tart. They shared out
the jam and cut the tart so that
everyone could have a piece.

Nearly everyone, that is.

"Not for me, thank you,"
said Slimpup politely. "I think
I've had more than my fair
share already."

Poorly Fat Puss

One windy day in spring, Fat Puss went to the park with the Mouse family. Robert and Charlotte had got some new paper kites and they wanted to try them out.

The kites flew well in the wind, and by the end of the afternoon everyone was exhausted from running up and down with them.

"Home time," said Terence at last, and they set off back. But as they walked along, the sky started to get darker and darker.

"Oh dear," said Jessica. "It looks like it's going to –"

Splish! A big raindrop fell on her nose.

"– rain."

Sure enough, a few moments later it was raining hard.

"We'll get soaked!" squeaked Robert.

"And our new kites will go soggy!" added Charlotte.

"Don't worry, everyone," said Terence. "I've brought an umbrella." He unfurled it quickly.

It was a lovely big red umbrella.

"Gosh," said Fat Puss admiringly. "I'd look forward to the rain if I had an umbrella like that."

The mice all scurried under it. "You too, Fat Puss," said Terence.

So Fat Puss leaned down one
way . . . and then the other.
But he couldn't fit under the
umbrella.

"You try holding it,"
suggested Jessica.
But that was no good either.

"Oh, I'll be fine without it,"
said Fat Puss bravely. "I've got
lots of fur, after all."

So the Mouse family huddled
together under the umbrella,
and Fat Puss followed behind.

By the time they all got home, Fat Puss was wet through. He was dripping so much that soon there was a puddle all round him.

"You do look funny, Fat Puss," giggled the Mouse children.

"I think I'd better go home and dry off," said Fat Puss.

The next morning, Terence
called to see Fat Puss. He
found him looking very
miserable.

"What's the matter?" asked
Terence.

"I'm not quite sure," said Fat Puss rather thickly. "My nose isn't working properly. It's all blocked up and I keep – ATISHOO! – I keep doing that."

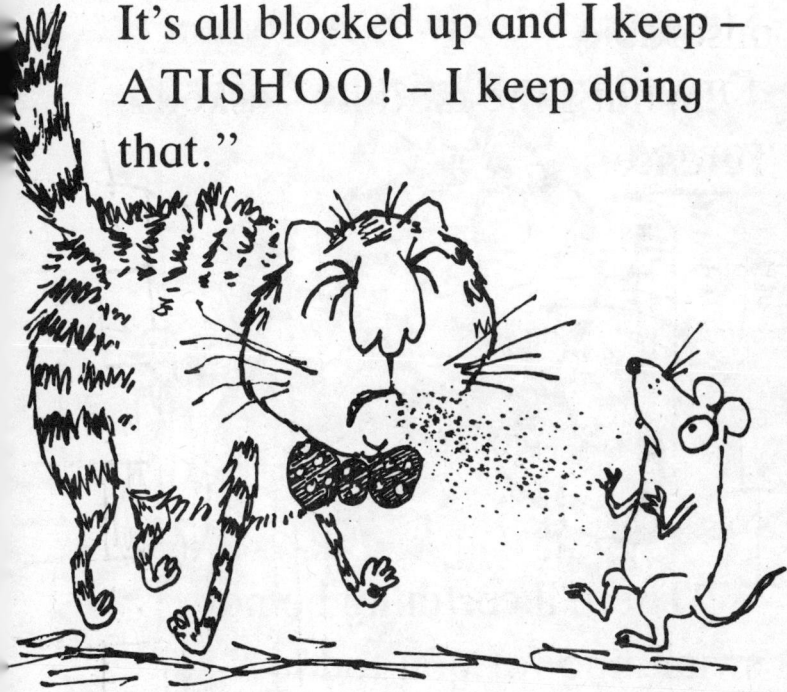

"Sneezing – oh dear," said Terence. "You've got a cold, Fat Puss. It sounds like you'd better go to bed."

"To bed?" said Fat Puss.
"But I can't. I'm supposed to
be going swimming with
Humphrey Beaver. And then
I'm going to Christine Crow's
for tea."

"There'll certainly be no
swimming for you today," said
Terence firmly. "And no tea at
Christine's either, I'm afraid.
You'll have to stay in bed until
you get better."

So Terence put Fat Puss to bed and tucked him up. Fat Puss lay there, sneezing into his handkerchief and thinking sadly of how lonely he was going to be, staying in bed all on his own.

He began to feel rather sorry for himself. "See you in a few days then, Terence," he said.

"What's that?" said Terence, surprised. "I'm not going anywhere, Fat Puss. I'm going to stay here and look after you."

"You are?" said Fat Puss. He began to feel better already.

In fact, Fat Puss found that
being ill wasn't lonely at all.
He not only had Terence
looking after him, bringing him
hot drinks and new
handkerchiefs, but all his other
friends took it in turns to come
and see him too.

The Mouse children brought
him a picture they had drawn.

The baby crows gave a flying
display to cheer him up and
make him laugh.

Humphrey told him news of
what was happening on the
river.

And Slimpup came and
made exciting plans for all the
things they would do when Fat
Puss was well again.

"I think you'd better stop bouncing up and down so much," laughed Terence. "Fat Puss will get tired and then he won't get better so quickly."

At last the day came when Fat Puss really was feeling better. The sneezing and snuffling had stopped and his nose was working properly once more.

Terence declared him officially well and allowed him to go out again.

Fat Puss felt very excited. After having his friends come to see him so much, he was really looking forward to going to visit them instead. He thanked Terence for looking after him, and then he set off.

"I'll visit Humphrey first,"
he said to himself. "Perhaps
he'd like to go for a swim."

But Humphrey wasn't there.

"Oh," said Fat Puss disappointedly. "Never mind. I'll call on Slimpup instead."

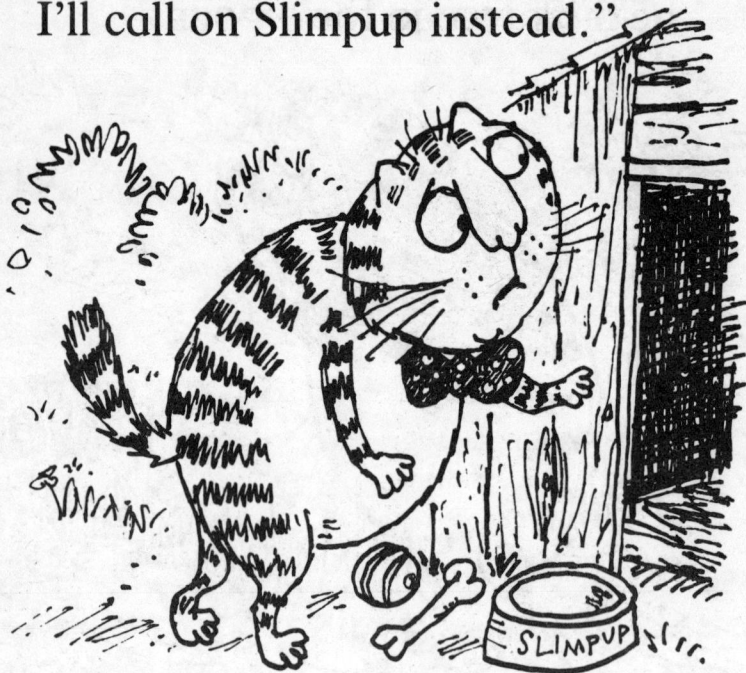

But Slimpup wasn't there either.

"Oh," said Fat Puss again. "Maybe the Mouse children are at home."

But they weren't. And there
was no sign of the Crow family
at their tree in the woods.

"Where can everybody be?"
wondered Fat Puss. "They
must have all gone off on a trip
without me."

He walked along sadly,
almost wishing he was ill again
just so that he could see his
friends. After a while he came
to the park, and wandered in.

Suddenly he heard a great
shout. "Surprise!" He looked
up, and saw all his friends
there, waiting for him.

"Welcome back, Fat Puss!"
said Humphrey Beaver.
"We've missed having you
around," said Christine Crow.

Everyone hugged Fat Puss.
"And we've all got you a
present," said Jessica, "to say
well done for getting better."
She handed him a big parcel.

"Open it! Open it!" chirped the baby birds excitedly. Fat Puss unwrapped the parcel. Inside he found a beautiful brand-new umbrella. It was bright red, just like Terence's, but much bigger.

"Oh, how lovely," said Fat
Puss. "Thank you so much."

"We thought you might be
needing it," smiled Terence.
"So that you don't get ill
EVERY time it rains."

Fat Puss's First Birthday

One morning, Fat Puss went to see the Mouse family. When he got there, he found that Slimpup was there too.

"I have an announcement to make," said Slimpup importantly.

"What is it?" asked Terence Mouse.

"It's my birthday today," said Slimpup.

"Is it? How lovely," said Fat Puss.

"Well, at least, I think it is,"
said Slimpup. "I definitely feel
older today than I did
yesterday – a whole birthday
older – so it must be."

"I wish I knew when my
birthday was," said Fat Puss.

"Why don't you have one today, with me?" suggested Slimpup. "We could have a joint birthday."

"Could we really?" asked Fat Puss. "Don't you mind not having a birthday all to yourself, Slimpup?"

"Not at all," said Slimpup.

"Well, if it's your joint birthday today," said Terence, "we must have a joint birthday party."

"Ooh yes!" said Slimpup, jumping up and down in excitement.

"But there's just one question," continued Terence. "How old are you?"

Slimpup stopped jumping up and down and looked puzzled. "How old are you, Fat Puss?" he asked.

Fat Puss thought hard and then shook his head. "I don't know," he said.

"Oh dear, neither do I," said Slimpup. "Does this mean that

we can't have our birthday
after all?"

"I'm sure we can work out
how old you are," said Jessica
Mouse. "Have you ever had a
birthday before?"

"I'm not sure," said Fat Puss. "How can you tell if it's your birthday?"

"You have a party," said Charlotte, "and a birthday cake."

"And people say 'Happy Birthday, Fat Puss!' to you," added Robert.

"No, I've never had a party
or a cake or a 'Happy Birthday,
Fat Puss!'" said Fat Puss.

"Neither have I," said
Slimpup.

"Well, in that case it must be
your first birthday," said
Jessica.

"Now that we've sorted that
out," said Terence, "we must
get ready for the party."

Terence went to find
Humphrey Beaver and
Christine Crow to tell them
about the party, while the
Mouse children ran off to make
the birthday cake, and Slimpup
went to help them. They made
a lot of mess, and Slimpup got
so excited that he kept falling
into the mixing bowl.

But eventually they got it
finished.

Meanwhile, Fat Puss helped
Jessica to make lots of brightly
coloured paper-chains, and
Christine and Grandma Crow
hung them on the trees.

Terence and Humphrey
Beaver made a big banner
saying HAPPY FIRST
BIRTHDAY FAT PUSS
AND SLIMPUP! and when
they had finished it Christine
and Grandma hung that on the
trees too.

When it was time for the
party, Katie, Lizzie and Kevin
Crow gave everyone the party
hats that they had made. Then
they played some games.

They played musical statues, but Slimpup wasn't very good at that because he was far too excited to keep still.

Then they tied a scarf
around Humphrey Beaver's
eyes and played blind-beaver's
buff. Slimpup wasn't very good
at that either, because he kept
squeaking, so Humphrey
always knew where he was.

Then they played hide-and-
seek. "May I seek please?"
asked Fat Puss. "Because I
always get found straight away
when I hide."

"Since it's your birthday,"
said Christine Crow, "of course
you can."

So Fat Puss closed his eyes
and counted, while the others
hid.

Then he started to look for
them. At first he couldn't see
anyone.

There was no one under the
bench.

And no one in the litter-bin.

Then he heard muffled giggles coming from the watering-can. He peered in, and found Slimpup, the Mouse children and the baby birds all squashed inside, hiding together.

When they had untangled
themselves, they all began to
look for the others. They found
Humphrey under a pile of
twigs, pretending to be a bush.

They found Jessica hiding
under an overturned spade.
Terence was hiding in the bird-
bath. And Christine and
Grandma Crow were hanging
upside-down from the birthday
banner, pretending to be bats.

"Oh, I'm glad you found us,"
said Grandma Crow. "I'm not
as good at that as I used to be."

When the games were over,
it was time to go home.

"Wait a minute!" said
Charlotte suddenly. "We've
forgotten something."

A moment later she and
Robert appeared with the
birthday cake. It had one
candle in the middle.

"Since it is your joint birthday," said Robert to Fat Puss and Slimpup, "you must blow out the candle together."

So Fat Puss and Slimpup breathed in and blew as hard as they could. The candle went out and everyone clapped.

"Happy Birthday, Fat Puss and Slimpup!" they cried.

"I've really enjoyed our birthday," said Fat Puss happily.

"So have I," said Slimpup. "In fact," he added, with his mouth full of birthday cake, "I think we should have one every year."

Also in Young Puffin

Fat Puss and Friends

Harriet Castor

Fat Puss was fat. He had little thin arms, small flat feet, a very short tail and an amazingly fat tummy.

He can't do all sorts of things that his friends can do, but instead of being miserable he finds some special (and funny) things he *can* do – like making friends with mice!

Also in Young Puffin

THE RAILWAY CAT

Phyllis Arkle

**Railway Porter v. Railway Cat.
Who will win?**

Alfie the railway cat lives at the station
where he's a favourite with all the
regular passengers. The only trouble is
that Hack, the new railway porter,
doesn't like cats and he soon has a plan
for getting rid of Alfie.

Also in Young Puffin

MRS COCKLE'S CAT

Philippa Pearce

Peter Cockle longs and longs for a mouthful of fresh fish.

One of the things that Mrs Cockle's cat, Peter, loves most in the world is fresh fish for tea. One summer the weather is so bad that the fishermen can't take their boats out to sea. Peter has to do something about the lack of fresh fish...and Mrs Cockle is left all alone.